Anansi at the Pool

Retold by Grace Hallworth

Illustrated by Sheila Moxley

Deep in the forest there was a pool of cool clear water. Every day, Monkey, Tortoise and Parrot went there to drink. It was their secret meeting place.

One morning they found the water in the pool all dirty and brown.

"Who has made our pool so muddy?" shrieked Parrot.

"Not I," said Monkey.

"Not I," said Tortoise.

"Well **someone** did!" said Parrot.

They searched everywhere but they saw no one. Nobody noticed Anansi the spider hiding up in the branches of a Poui tree with beautiful blossoms.

On the very next day when the
animals visited the pool the water
was even more muddy than before.

"Someone comes to our pool at night.
We must find out who it is," said
Parrot. "Who will keep
watch with
me tonight?"

"I will," said Monkey.

"I will," said Tortoise.
So the three friends waited and
watched to see who would come.
They saw no one, but in the morning
the pool was muddy again.

All that day the animals stayed near
the pool. They thought and they
thought about what they should do.

At last Tortoise said, "I think I know
of a way to catch the one who comes
at night." The others gathered around
to hear Tortoise's plan.

 "Smear some of the sticky stuff from
the gum tree over my back. And
when it gets dark, place me near the
stepping stones at the edge of the pool,"
said Tortoise.
So they did.

 Later that night Tortoise heard a
gentle tip, tap, tip, tap coming along
the path. He peered into the darkness
but he could not see anyone.

Tip, tap, tip, tap, tip,tap, the sounds
were getting nearer and nearer.
Then Tortoise felt soft fine legs
climbing onto his back. He felt
soft fine legs moving over his
back and then, held fast to his back.
 "Who's that sitting on my back?"
asked Tortoise.

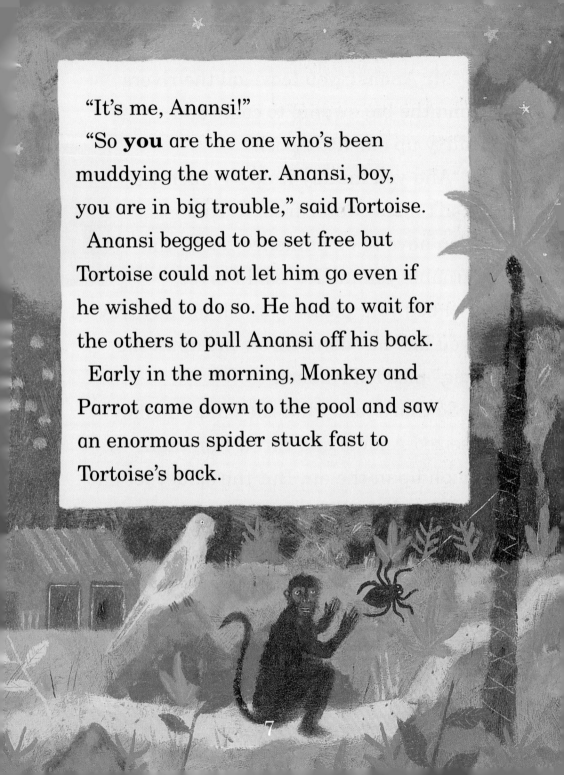

"It's me, Anansi!"

"So **you** are the one who's been muddying the water. Anansi, boy, you are in big trouble," said Tortoise.

Anansi begged to be set free but Tortoise could not let him go even if he wished to do so. He had to wait for the others to pull Anansi off his back.

Early in the morning, Monkey and Parrot came down to the pool and saw an enormous spider stuck fast to Tortoise's back.

"Oho!" exclaimed Monkey,

"Mr Anansi, you leave all the rivers
and the big swamp to come and
dirty up our little pool!"

"And you muddy it up so much we
can't drink water from it! Anansi,
you have to be punished for all the
trouble you made," said Parrot.

"I beg you, please, punish me any way
you like but don't throw me up in the
air," pleaded Anansi.

So that's just what they did. Monkey
seized Anansi and threw him high,
high up in the air. But the spider let out
a strand of silken thread and swung far,
far out until he touched the bark of a
tree. There he anchored his thread and
ran and hid in its branches.

And that is where you'll find him to
this day.